Bugs Bunny Marooned!

By
JUSTINE KORMAN

Illustrated by
JOE MESSERLI

A GOLDEN BOOK • NEW YORK
Western Publishing Company, Inc., Racine, Wisconsin 53404

Bugs Bunny was a happy stowaway among the carrot crates on Yosemite Sam's ship. But the ornery captain was not happy to find Bugs there.

"Get off and stay off, ye fur-bearin' critter!" Yosemite Sam shouted, tossing Bugs into a tiny lifeboat.

And Bugs was set adrift, with only a carrot for an oar.

Bugs knew that sailors steer by the stars. "Now, let's see," he said. "North Star over here. Orion's Belt over there. According to my calculations, my rabbit hole should be right about there!"

Bugs started to row.

The next morning he reached the sandy shore of a desert island. "This doesn't look like home," Bugs said, looking around. "But it sure beats bouncing around in that little boat."

Bugs sat down to eat his one and only carrot.

Then Bugs set out to search for more food and fresh water. He wandered into the jungle, and there he noticed something strange—everything was much, much bigger than normal size.

"Hey, I've seen pigeons smaller than that butterfly!" he exclaimed. "And get a load of those violets!"

"Is this a mirage, or am I in heaven?" Bugs wondered when he saw a gigantic carrot.

He tugged and tugged as hard as he could, but that carrot would not budge.

Then Bugs had an idea. He bent a sapling and tied the carrot top to its branches. Then he let the tree spring straight again. The carrot popped out of the ground.

Bugs had hardly taken two bites when a strange little man in a white coat stepped into the clearing.

"What's up, doc?" Bugs asked.

"Actually, I am not a doctor. I am Professor Ex, a research scientist studying accelerated growth in organic life forms," the man replied.

"Is that so?" Bugs asked between bites. "Was this carrot your idea?"

"Yes," said the man, rubbing his hands together. "I was hoping to trap something tasty with it. And here you are."

"Tasty?" Bugs asked, chomping nervously on the giant carrot.

"Yes," said Professor Ex, licking his lips. "I am so tired of coconut soup, coconut custard, coconut milk shakes. What I need is a nice rabbit stew."

"Well, I hate to eat and run, doc," Bugs said as he started to run away. But his feet only scraped the ground. Bugs was being held fast by a mechanical arm that telescoped out of the professor's pocket.

Soon Bugs was the professor's prisoner.
"Struggle all you want, yummy thing. The Acme
Portable Bubble Cage is guaranteed escape-proof,"
Professor Ex cackled.

In his laboratory, the professor got ready to make the rabbit stew.

"Listen, doc," Bugs said. "Since you're going to all this trouble, why don't you make me big, too? Then you can have rabbit salad sandwiches tomorrow, rabbit noodle casserole, rabbit tomato surprise..."

"Such cleverness from a lower mammal!" the professor said. "Hold still while I focus the growth ray."

Bugs grew so big that he burst the bubble cage.
"Oh, dear, what have I done?" Professor Ex fretted as
the enormous bunny bounded away.

"Bring me the rabbit, Malcolm," the professor commanded his giant dog. "And be quick. The ray only flashed on him for a moment, and it may wear off soon. I want to cook him while he is still big."

"Bow wow, wow, wow!" Malcolm barked.

Bugs was running through the forest. Suddenly the ground beneath him began to shake. The air was filled with the wild barking of the professor's dog.

"What's up, dog?" Bugs asked.

"Bow wow, wow!" Malcolm barked.

"Oh, I get it," Bugs said. "You're bringing your master his rabbit." Bugs blinked his eyes. "Rabbit?!"

Bugs needed a way to escape. "Say, what's that on your shoulder?" he asked Malcolm.

Malcolm only growled.

"Not falling for that old trick?" Bugs asked. "Go ahead, let it crawl up your neck. See if I care."

When the dog turned to look over his shoulder, Bugs
jumped away, kicking Malcolm with his big hind feet.
"What a dope!" Bugs laughed. "Fell for the old
over- the-shoulder trick!"

Suddenly Bugs heard the sound of giant wings. He turned just in time to see a tremendous owl about to pluck him up in its terrible claws.

"Uh oh," said Bugs. "Owls eat rabbits."

Bugs looked down and saw Malcolm chasing after them. That gave him an idea. "Say, doc," he said to the owl. "Why would you want a skinny old rabbit when there's a plump, juicy dog right over there?"

From way up high, Malcolm looked small enough to grab. The owl dropped Bugs and swooped after the dog.

"I feel funny," Bugs thought as he fell down into the trees. When he saw the giant carrot again, he knew why. The growth ray had worn off, and he was a normal-sized rabbit again.

"I'd better get out of here before someone else tries to get me," Bugs said. "But I'm not leaving this carrot behind."

Bugs dragged the giant carrot to the shore. He was wondering how to get home with it when he heard buzzing overhead. A giant mosquito flew out of the woods.

Bugs knotted the carrot greens into a lasso. He nabbed the huge mosquito and tied it to his carrot.

Bugs pushed the carrot into the water. When he saw that it would float, he climbed aboard. The mosquito's flapping wings made a speedy outboard motor.

"This thing is a great boat," Bugs said, taking a bite as they sped away. "I just hope I don't finish it before we get home."